# DON'T DO THAT!

## by Tony Ross

Andersen Press • London

Copyright © 1991 by Tony Ross
First published in 1991 by Andersen Press Ltd., 20 Vauxhall Bridge Road, London SW1V 2SA. Published in Australia by Random Century Australia Pty., Ltd., 20 Alfred Street, Milsons Point, Sydney, NSW 2061. All rights reserved. Colour separated in Switzerland by Photolitho AG, Gossau, Zürich. Printed and bound in Italy by Grafiche AZ, Verona.

10 9 8 7 6 5 4 3 2 1

British Library Cataloguing in Publication Data available.

ISBN 0-86264-344-9

Nellie had a pretty nose.

It was so pretty that it won pretty nose competitions.

It was so pretty that Nellie was given a part in the
Christmas play, with Donna and Patricia, who had pretty
noses too.

"CHILDREN, don't do that!" said teacher.

"It won't come out, sir," said Nellie. "It's *stuck*."

The teacher tried to get Nellie's finger out, but he couldn't.

Neither could the head teacher.
"It's stuck," they said, and sent Nellie home.

"It's stuck," said Nellie.
"I can get it out," said Henry.
"Mum," shouted Nellie.

But Mum couldn't get Nellie's finger out.
"I can," said Henry.

So Mum called the doctor.
"I can't get it out," he said.
"I can," said Henry.

So the doctor called the police.
"We can't get it out," they said.
"I can," said Henry.

So the police called the conjurer.
"I can't get it out," he said.
"I can," said Henry.

So the conjurer called the farmer.
"I can't get it out," said the farmer.
"I can," said Henry.

So the farmer called the fire brigade.
"We can't get it out," they said.
"I can," said Henry.

Nobody could get Nellie's finger out.
Her nose was longer, and it hurt.
There was only one thing left to do.

"I can get it out," said Henry.

So everybody called the scientist.
"Of course I can get it out," he said . . .

... "Science can do anything."
And he measured Nellie's nose.
"I can get it out," said Henry.

So the scientist built a rocket ship, and tied it to Nellie's arm.

Then he tied Nellie's leg to the park bench.

Then he set off the rocket,

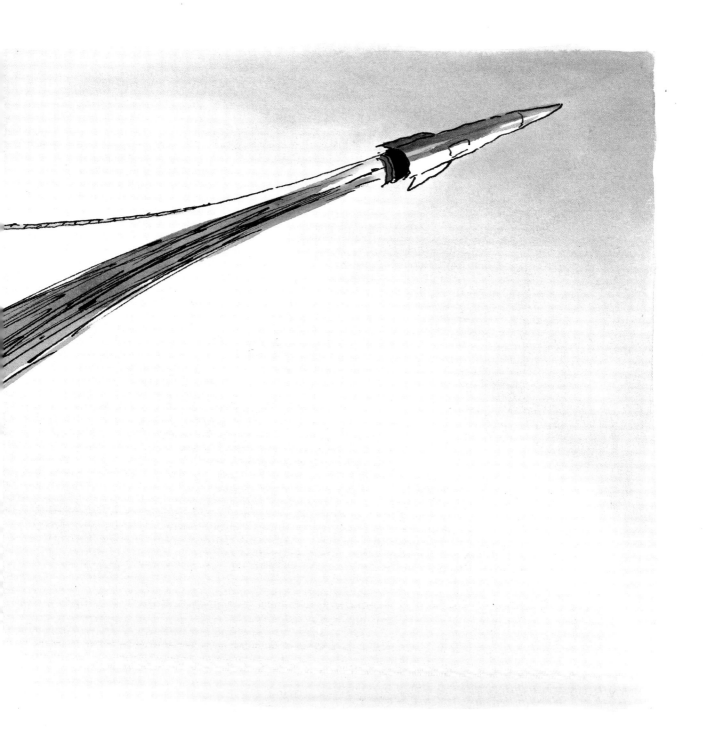

. . . but Nellie's finger *still* wouldn't come out.

"I can get it out," said Henry.

"Go on then!" said the teachers, Mum, the doctor, the police, the conjurer, the farmer, the fire brigade and the scientist.

So Henry tickled Nellie...
...and it worked!

The end →